To my mother, Roberta Loomis, and her dreams

C. L.

For Danny, Rama, and little Tomer with love

O. E.

ISBN 0-590-03373-5

12 11 10 9 8 7 6 5 4 3 2 1   9/9 0 1 2 3 4/0

Printed in the U.S.A.   24

First Scholastic printing, March 1999

The art was done in gouache on plywood panels.
Designed by Gunta Alexander. Text set in Friz Quadrata.

COWBOY BUNNIES

Christine Loomis
pictures by Ora Eitan

SCHOLASTIC INC.
New York   Toronto   London   Auckland   Sydney
Mexico City   New Delhi   Hong Kong

Cowboy bunnies

Wake up early

Ride their ponies

Hurly burly

Start at sunup
Work all day
Roping cows
Tossing hay

Mending fences
On the ridges
Jumping gullies
Fixing bridges

Bronco busters
In the saddle
Whoop and holler
Count the cattle

Cowboy bunnies
On the ground
Start the campfire
Gather round

Ring the lunch bell
Rub their bellies
Eat up flapjacks
Eggs and jellies

Steak and 'taters   Corn and cake

Bunnies get   A bellyache

Cowboy bunnies
Feeling hot
Find a cool
And shady spot

Chase each other
Sit and doze
Roll their pants up
Dip their toes

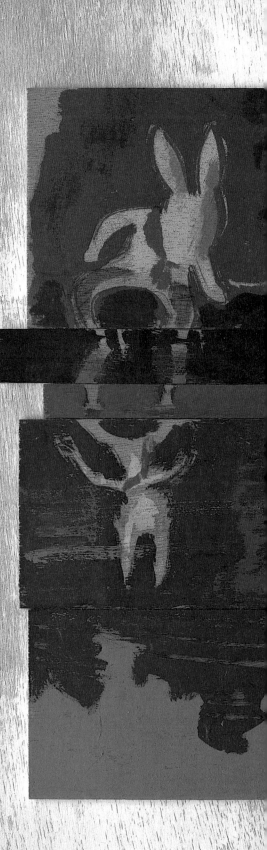

Call their ponies
Hit the trail
Over hill
And over dale

Till their work
Is finally done
Then the bunnies
Have some fun

Cowboy bunnies
Big and little
Pick a banjo
Play a fiddle

Grab a partner
Little or big
Dance to the music
Jiggity jig

Sing a lonesome
Cowboy tune
Underneath a
Silver moon

Stay up late   Home they go

Rub their eyes   With sleepy sighs

Cowboy bunnies   In pajamas   Hug and kiss

Their cowboy mamas

Mamas sing
Sweet lullabies
Papas softly
Harmonize

Stars are twinkling
Stars are bright
Cowboy bunnies
Say good night